WHAT

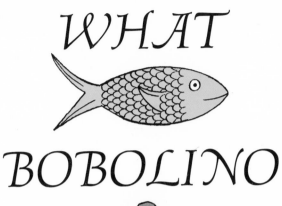

BOBOLINO

KNEW

by Anne Rockwell

THE McCALL PUBLISHING COMPANY · NEW YORK

for Marilyn

Copyright©1971 by Anne Rockwell
All rights reserved. Published simultaneously
in Canada by Doubleday Canada Ltd., Toronto.
Library of Congress Catalog Card Number: 72–135442
SBN8415-2027–5. First printing. Printed in the
United States of America. The McCall Publishing
Company, 230 Park Avenue, New York, N. Y. 10017

On a faraway island there lived a rich and bad-tempered nobleman who had but one son, who was named Bobolino.

Bobolino was as friendly and cheerful as his father was
gloomy and grouchy, and for this reason his father thought
him a little stupid. But all the same, he decided to send
Bobolino across the sea to study foreign languages with
a wise teacher, for, as he said:

2

"A man who could speak French, Chinese, Latin, Arabic,
and Greek would surely *seem* clever, even if he were not."

Years went by and at last Bobolino returned home.
"Say something to me in French!" his father commanded,
 even before he had said "hello."
 But Bobolino, smiling cheerfully, said:
"I know no French."
"Well, in that case, let me hear you speak Chinese,"
 his father said.

But Bobolino said:
"I know no words of Chinese."
His father sputtered and grew red in the face.
"Arabic?" he roared.

But Bobolino shook his head and smiled.
"I know no French, no Chinese, no Latin, no Arabic,
and not one word of Greek. But I can tell you what the
cricket on the window sill is saying."

As his father sat speechless with anger, Bobolino
explained that his master had thought it best to begin
by teaching him the languages of animals before he taught
him the languages of men.
"I can understand the crickets, the birds, the frogs and
toads, all the friendly beasts of field and farm, and even
the fishes in the sea," he said proudly.

Hearing this, Bobolino's father grew even angrier. He stamped out of the room, slamming doors and kicking chairs as he marched down the hall, grunting and snorting in fury.

Bobolino felt very sad, for he had so hoped his father
would be proud of him. With a heavy heart, he went to
his room. There he saw a little bird sitting upon his
night table. Bobolino greeted the bird politely, but the
bird answered:

"I have just flown from your father's courtyard. He is so
ashamed of you that he wants to lock you up in his
dungeon and never set you free. I have heard him planning
it with his jailer."

Although Bobolino loved his father and wished that he could please him, the bird convinced him that he must run away. He climbed out through his window and headed for the nearby hills as the little bird wished him good fortune and flew off into the sky.

Night came and Bobolino stretched out to sleep at the edge of a small pond. He had no sooner closed his eyes, however, when he heard loud and excited croaking coming from the frogs in the pond. In a moment he was wide awake and listening carefully to what the frogs were saying. Then, quickly and quietly, he ran off.

In two minutes he reached a farmyard, where there was
a large pen filled with sheep. The lights were out in the
farmhouse, but Bobolino knocked loudly at the door and
the sleepy farmer opened it.

"Robbers are coming to steal your sheep!" Bobolino whispered to the farmer. "Take a stick, and follow me to the frog pond."

Because Bobolino had such a pleasant, friendly face, the farmer trusted him and followed.

No sooner had the two of them reached the frog pond than they began to shout: "Come out robbers, wherever you are!" and thrash the air with two strong sticks they were carrying.

And very soon, two mean-faced fellows jumped out of the bushes and ran away as fast as they could go.

"Thank you," said the farmer to Bobolino. "Tell me, how did you know they were there?"

Bobolino was too shy to tell the farmer that he understood the language of frogs, so he just shrugged his shoulders and said nothing.

Next morning, after spending a comfortable night in the farmhouse, Bobolino rode off on a donkey the grateful farmer had given him.

After a while Bobolino and his donkey passed another donkey and rider along the path.

"Good day, friend," said Bobolino's donkey. "How are things in the city today?"

"Ahhhhhh...not good, not good," the other donkey replied, with a long, sad sigh. "The king, who is so old, is very sick, and some say that he will die before the week is up. I heard this from my cousin, who delivers vegetables to the palace kitchen."

"And who will be king, if he dies?" asked Bobolino's
   donkey.
"There is no one. The king, as you know, has no children.
   He has never found a man wise enough to rule after him,
   although he has spent his long life looking and listening
   for one."

With this news the donkeys said good-bye to each other
and went on their way, not knowing that Bobolino had
overheard their conversation.

The noonday sun was hot and high, so Bobolino and his donkey headed down toward the cool, blue sea. Bobolino fed the donkey three ripe figs he had brought along for his lunch. Then he went for a swim. The sea was calm; the water was clear and bright; the sky was blue, and there was not a cloud to be seen. A big fish poked his head above the water and peered curiously at Bobolino.

"Good day, friend fish," said Bobolino, and the fish was very surprised to hear a person speak to him. Bobolino began to tell the fish the story of how his father had sent him away to learn the many languages of men, and how, instead, he had learned the languages of beasts. But suddenly, in the middle of the story, the fish interrupted Bobolino and said with a frown:
"Leave this water right away! I must tell you, a great storm is coming from the east. We fish can hide in the deep water where it is always quiet. But alas, you, my friend, cannot come down there with us."

Bobolino thanked the fish for this news and quickly swam back to the sandy beach.

Not far off he saw a little fishing boat setting out to sea,
and he said to the donkey:

"Come quickly! A storm is coming, and we must warn the
fishermen, so that their boats will not be wrecked at sea,
and none of the fishermen will be drowned."

The donkey was so surprised to hear Bobolino talk in
donkey talk that he said nothing, but instead raced off
with Bobolino on his back faster than any donkey had
ever trotted before. In no time at all they reached the
city where lay the fishing port, lined with bright-colored
boats.

Bobolino went from fisherman to fisherman, warning them of the coming storm, but none of them would listen to him. They went on putting their big nets into their little boats, for as one old fisherman said:
"Look at the sea. It is clear and blue; not a cloud is in the sky; the wind is calm, and there is no storm in sight. I know, I have fished these waters for many years, while you are a stranger and no fisherman, as I can see by your clothes."

Just as Bobolino was sure that no one would listen to him,
the farmer whose sheep had almost been stolen came along
the dock on his way to the marketplace. When he heard
Bobolino talking excitedly to the fishermen, he said
to them:

"Listen to him. Last night he told me that robbers were
waiting to steal my sheep, and he was right. I saw them
after he warned me, and the two of us chased them away."
When they heard this the fishermen said to one another:
"Perhaps he is right. We will stay at home today and mend
our nets."

As suddenly as it began, the storm was over. All of the
people came into the market square. Each one of them had
heard, from each one's neighbor, of how the stranger,
Bobolino, had saved the fishermen from the storm, and
how he had told the farmer of the robbers.

"Surely," each person said to one another, "surely *this* man
is wise enough to be our king!"

So they gave Bobolino the crown.

He ruled wisely and well, with the help of the birds,

and the rabbits, and the fish in the sea, and the sheep and donkeys of the farms and fields.

Anne Rockwell has been writing and illustrating children's books for the past ten years. Among her books are *Fillippo's Dome, The Wonderful Eggs of Furicchia,* and *Savez Vous Planter Les Choux.*

She is married to Harlow Rockwell, who is also an illustrator and designer, and the Rockwells have collaborated on several science books for very young children.

The Rockwells enjoy traveling and have spent many vacations in Europe, especially France and Italy. They now live in Old Greenwich, Connecticut, with their three children.